When the Snow Falls

Linda Booth Sweeney • illustrated by Jana Christy

SCHOLASTIC INC.

For my snow buddies—Anna, Nancy and Gale.
—LBS

For my family, who loves snowy days as much as I do.
—JC

ISBN 978-1-338-35766-0

12 11 10 9 8 7 6 5 4 3 2 1   18 19 20 21 22 23

Printed in the U.S.A.   169

First Scholastic printing, November 2018

Design by Dave Kopka
Text set in ITC Goudy Sans and Modern Love
The images were created using pencil sketches and mixed media, assembled and painted digitally.

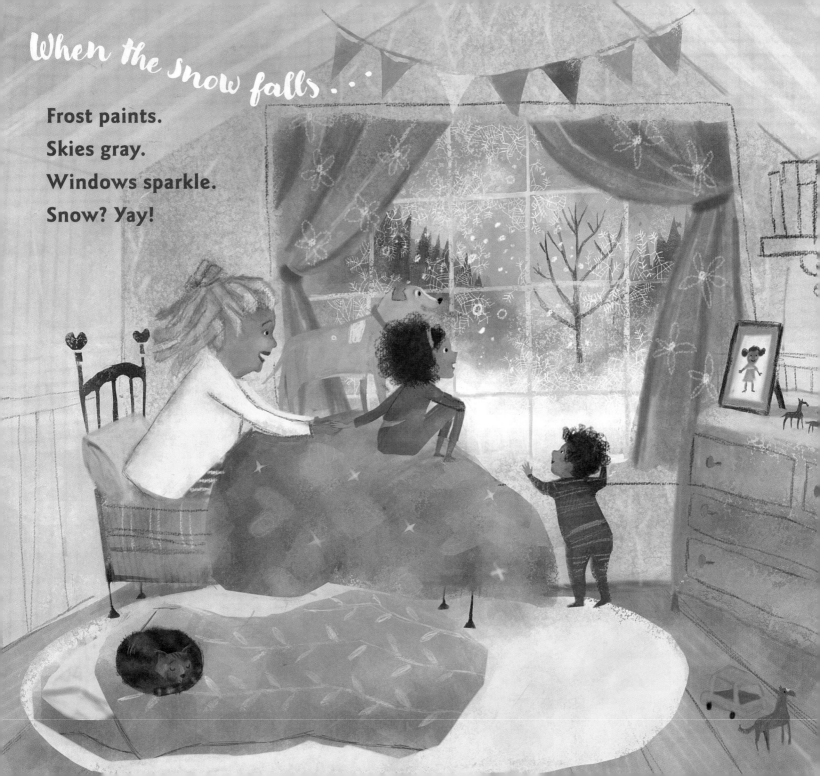

When the snow falls...

Frost paints.
Skies gray.
Windows sparkle.
Snow? Yay!

Grandma zips.
Daddy tugs.
Belts buckle.
Hats snug.

Boots sink.
Lashes flick.
Tongues tickle.
We lick.

Barn creaks.
Horses neigh.
Bells tinkle.
Puppies play.

When the snow falls . . .

Tracks curve.
Skis glide.
Fox curls.
Rabbits hide.

Woods *hush*.
Fields glisten.
Wren sings.
We listen.

When the snow falls . . .

Trains toot.
Cars slow.
Plows push.
Mountains grow.

Wheels *crunch*.
Shovels scoop.
Ice *cracks!*
Awnings droop.

Flakes zag.
Flakes zig.
Grandpa whistles.
We dig.

Balls roll.
Mounds pile.
Carrots stick.
Snowmen smile.

Saucers spin.
Sleds slide.
Hats fly.
We ride!

Friends flop.
Snow creeps.
We *swish*.
Angels sleep.

When the snow falls . . .

Toes tingle.
Lips quiver.
Cheeks glow.
We shiver.

Bones chill.
Winds chase.
Grandma calls.
We race!

Fire crackles.
Corn pops.
Soup simmers.
We plop.

Cocoa warms.
Mittens puddle.
Day dawdles.
We cuddle.